USE YOUR IMAGINATION

For Kate, Louise, Kristina, Steph and Vicki – thank you.
N.O.

First published 2014 by Nosy Crow Ltd
The Crow's Nest, 10a Lant Street,
London SE1 1QR
www.nosycrow.com

This edition first published 2015

ISBN 978 0 85763 335 4 (HB)
ISBN 978 0 85763 392 7 (PB)

Nosy Crow and associated logos are trademarks
and/or registered trademarks of Nosy Crow Ltd.

Text and illustrations copyright © Nicola O'Byrne 2014

The right of Nicola O'Byrne to be identified as the
author and illustrator of this work has been asserted.

A CIP catalogue record for this book is available from the British Library.

Printed in China
Papers used by Nosy Crow are made from wood grown
in sustainable forests.

3 5 7 9 8 6 4 2 (HB)
1 3 5 7 9 8 6 4 2 (PB)

USE YOUR IMAGINATION

Nicola O'Byrne

nosy crow

One day, Rabbit
was feeling bored.
"I wish **something** would happen,"
he said.

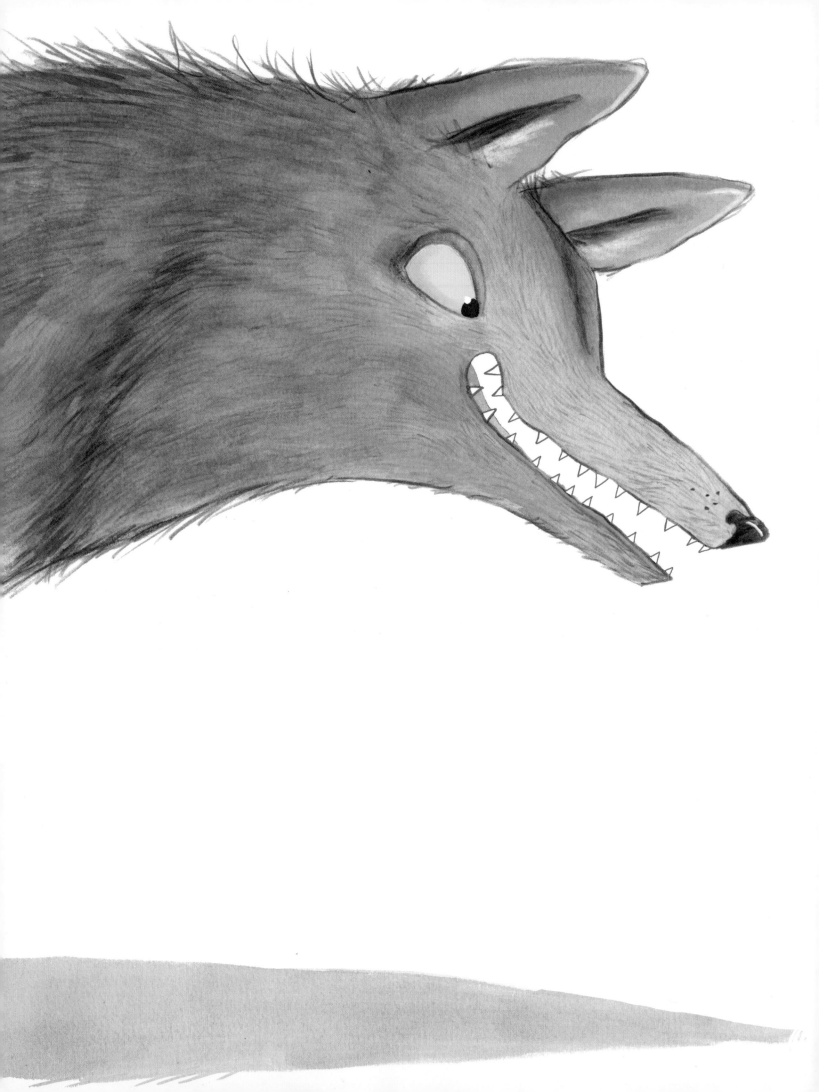

"Excuse me,"

said a voice. "May I help?"

It was Wolf.

"Well, maybe . . ." said Rabbit. "I'm **bored.**"

"Why don't we write a story?"
said Wolf. "I am a **librarian**, you know,
and librarians know a **lot**
about stories."

"You don't **look** like a librarian," said Rabbit.
"What **big ears** you've got!"

"All the better for **listening to stories** with,
my dear," said Wolf.

"And what **big eyes** you've got!"
said Rabbit.

"All the better for **reading** with,
my dear," said Wolf.

"Hmmm, I'm sure I've heard something like that before,"
said Rabbit.

"Never mind that," said Wolf quickly.
"Let's get on with the story."

"But how do we start?"
asked Rabbit.

"You need to

USE YOUR IMAGINATION!

It's making up *words* and pictures in your head to tell a story," explained Wolf. "And, of course, there's really only **one** way to begin a story . . .

 **ONCE UPON A TIME!"**

"But **what** is our story going to be about?"
asked Rabbit.

"Well," said Wolf. **"USE YOUR IMAGINATION."**

"Space rockets!" cried Rabbit. **"BIG** explosions!!
And bananas. We need LOTS of bananas!!!"

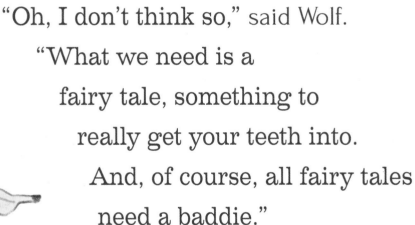

"Oh, I don't think so," said Wolf.
"What we need is a
fairy tale, something to
really get your teeth into.
And, of course, all fairy tales
need a baddie."

"What about a mouse?"
asked Rabbit.

"I was thinking about
something **bigger,"**
said Wolf.

"An **elephant!**" cried Rabbit.

"How about something
medium-sized?"
said Wolf, quickly.

"I know! What about **you?**"
asked Rabbit.

"Now, **that's**
a good idea,"
said Wolf.

"What next?" asked Rabbit.

"Well, of course, we need a hero," said Wolf.

"Me, me, me!" said Rabbit.

"What a great idea!" said Wolf.

"But what will I wear?" said Rabbit.

"Oh, it doesn't matter much," said Wolf. **"USE YOUR IMAGINATION."**

"A **SPACE SUIT!**" cried Rabbit. "Or a **pirate's hat!** Or . . . what about a little red cape?"

"Oh, you probably
don't need a thing,"
smiled Wolf.

"But where does this story happen?" asked Rabbit.

"USE YOUR IMAGINATION," said Wolf.

"That's a tricky one," said Rabbit.

"What do **you** think?"

"I was thinking of somewhere . . . tree-y," said Wolf.

"Oh, what about a **forest?**" squeaked Rabbit.

"Now, that's a good idea," said Wolf.

Rabbit felt very proud. "We've got a baddie, a hero
AND a forest," he said. "Is the story going to start soon?"

"Oh, yes," said Wolf, grinning. "The story starts . . .

. . . **RIGHT NOW!"**

as Wolf

chased after

him.

"Really?" snarled Wolf.
"Well, don't worry.
We're nearly
at the
end."

"I don't think so,"
said Rabbit, suddenly stopping.
**"I'm the hero, after all . . .
and I'm going to**

USE MY IMAGINATION!"

And so . . .

. . . Rabbit did.

"This *isn't* a good idea **AT ALL**," said Wolf.

"Really?" grinned Rabbit. "Well, don't worry, we're nearly at the **end.**"

5, 4, 3, 2, 1 . . .

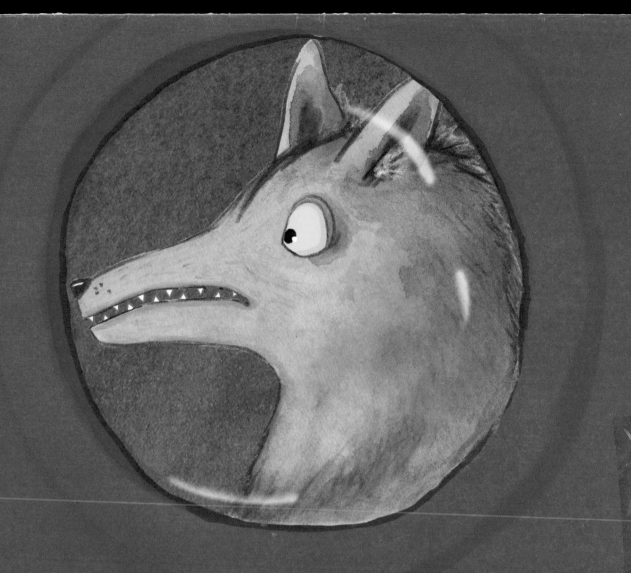

LIFT
UP

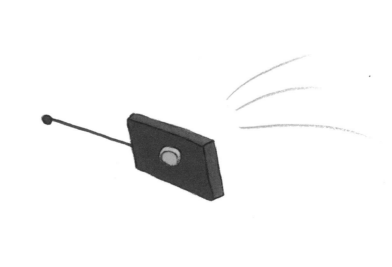

"Now **that** was
a good idea,"
said Rabbit . . .

"Isn't **IMAGINATION** a wonderful thing?"

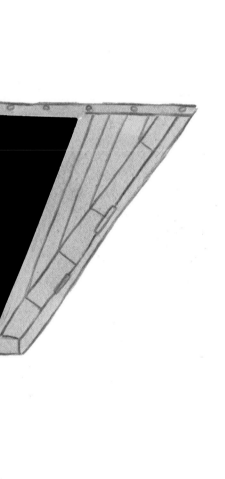

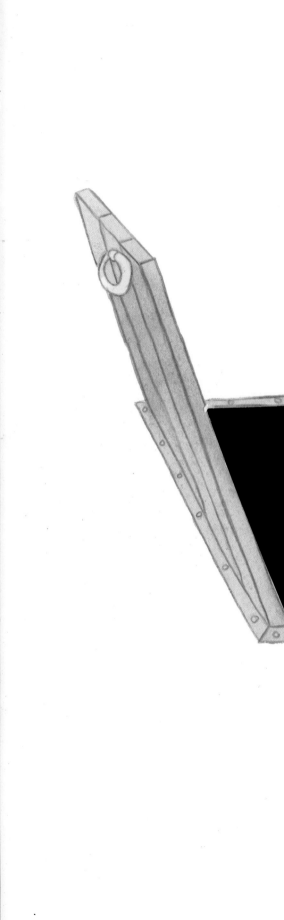